To the memory of Wick Wright,
grandnephew of Wilbur and Orville,
friend, gentleman, guardian of
the Wright family history —T. R. G.

To Marion, Leo, Josephine,
Clara, and Samuel —B. P.

Wee AND THE WRIGHT BROTHERS

TIMOTHY R. GAFFNEY ILLUSTRATED BY BERNADETTE PONS

HENRY HOLT AND COMPANY · NEW YORK

THE YEAR 1903 was a wonderful time to be a mouse. Wee thought so anyway. Wee was a mouse. He and Mama Mouse lived with their two mousekins in a bicycle shop in Dayton, Ohio. On a small printing press above the shop they published the *Mouse News*, a newspaper for mice in the neighborhood. Wee wrote the stories, Mama ran the press, and their little ones sold the papers.

Wee enjoyed living in the bicycle shop. He was a curious mouse, and the shop was full of fascinating things—fast-looking bicycle frames, shiny wheels, and the aromas of steel, rubber, and oil.

Two brothers named Wilbur and Orville Wright owned the shop. They made beautiful bicycles. "They work quietly and with great skill," Wee reported in the *Mouse News*. "They are also very fussy about neatness and even wear suits while they work."

The bicycles were interesting, but what intrigued Wee most were the flying machines Wilbur and Orville built in the back room of their shop. Going fast on a bicycle was not enough for them. They wanted to do what people in those days only dreamed of—they wanted to fly.

First they built a kite, then gliders big enough to carry one of them at a time. Every year they took a trip to test their gliders at a place called Kitty Hawk, far away in North Carolina.

The Wright brothers didn't tell many people about their attempts to fly. But whenever they discussed it between themselves in the shop, Wee was all ears. His mouse friends got the latest details in the *Mouse News.*

Now the brothers were making the most wonderful flying machine of all. It had a wooden frame and wings covered with white cloth. It also had something the gliders did not— a motor and two wooden propellers.

"The Wrights believe this powered machine will allow them to fly through the air like a bird," Wee reported. "They call it the *Flyer.*"

One day late in the summer, Wilbur and Orville began packing the *Flyer* into a wooden crate. Wee's little heart skipped a beat. "They're getting ready to go to Kitty Hawk," he told his family. "If only I could go and watch them fly. What a story it would make."

Wee looked at Mama and his mousekins, who watched him eagerly. "I will go!" he declared. "It will make the greatest *Mouse News* story ever!"

On the night before the Wrights set out, Wee's family helped him build a little nest in the *Flyer*'s crate. Mama packed bits of cheese and biscuit for the trip.

Wee kissed Mama and hugged the little ones. "I will miss you," he said. "I'll come home just as soon as I can."

As the Wright brothers loaded the crate onto a train bound for North Carolina, Wee settled into his cozy nest. He had never been on a train before. The crate rocked gently as the train rolled down the tracks. Wee drifted off to sleep.

When Wee awoke, they were on the coast of North Carolina. Kitty Hawk was a small village on an island. The Wright brothers put the crate onto a boat. Wee had never been on a boat either. He felt it pitching and rolling on the waves. His tummy felt it, too.

Wee was glad when they reached Kitty Hawk. Wilbur and Orville had a camp on a flat stretch of sand outside the village. When they got there, Wee slipped out and hid in their cabin.

Just as in the bicycle shop, the Wright brothers
kept everything neat. Wee tried to be neat, but a mouse
cannot help leaving crumbs here and there. The fussy
Wrights noticed.

Orville especially did not like having a mouse in the cabin.
He called Wee a "beastie" and chased him with a broom.
He made clever traps and baited them with crusty pieces
of cornbread. But Wee was quicker than Orville's broom,
and he knew every hiding place. He learned how to slip
the cornbread from Orville's traps without getting caught.

Wilbur and Orville had more to do than chase a mouse. They built a new shed for the *Flyer*. Then they started putting the *Flyer* together inside the shed.

Summer turned to autumn. The weather grew cold. Wee missed his family. Every morning, he hoped this would be the day for the *Flyer* to get off the ground.

On December 17, a freezing wind whistled through cracks in the cabin. But Wilbur and Orville were determined to fly. Some men from Kitty Hawk helped them pull the *Flyer* out of its shed.

Wee watched from the warm cabin through a small hole in the wall. He, too, wished he could fly.

The men set the *Flyer* on a wooden track. It was ready to go. Orville would make the first flight. But the men were shivering with cold. They came inside to warm up, took off their coats, and gathered around the hot stove.

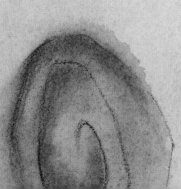

Wee wanted to fly so badly! And then he saw his chance.
While the men faced the stove, he sneaked into a pocket of
Orville's coat.

The men put on their coats and went outside again. Wee
burrowed deeply into Orville's pocket, where he stayed warm
and hidden.

The *Flyer* sat on its track, facing the wind. A strong wire held it in place. Orville took his position, lying belly down on the bottom wing. The motor started. Its valves chattered, its drive chains clattered, and the whole *Flyer* shook as its propellers began to whirl.

Wee crept out of the pocket. The wind was bitterly cold, but he had to see what was happening. He grabbed a strut near Orville and held on tight.

Orville released the wire. The propellers pushed the *Flyer* forward into the wind. Wilbur ran alongside, holding a wingtip to balance the machine until it lifted off the track.

Wee watched the ground drop away, and his little heart skipped two beats. "We're flying!" he squealed.

Orville didn't notice his tiny passenger. He was too busy working the controls.

ONE SECOND, TWO SECONDS, THREE SECONDS. . . .

Wee watched wide-eyed as the sandy ground rolled below. The *Flyer* was riding on nothing but air.

SIX SECONDS, SEVEN SECONDS, EIGHT SECONDS. . . .

Orville worked the controls as the *Flyer* bucked in the gusty wind.

ELEVEN SECONDS, TWELVE SECONDS—***THUD!***

The *Flyer* hit the ground. The hard landing threw Wee onto the sand. He was not hurt, but his little mouse head was spinning. "We must have crashed! What a disaster!" he thought.

But the *Flyer* was fine. The men were cheerful as they carried it back to the track and set it up for another flight. Wilbur went next, and his flight went farther. Orville flew again, and he went farther still. Wilbur took another turn and flew the farthest yet. After the fourth flight, a gust of wind caught the machine and smashed it.

The brothers were happy—they had built a machine that could fly under its own power. Their next flyer would be even better.

Wee was happy, too. What a feeling it had been to fly, and what a story he had for his newspaper! Now he could go home.

Back in Dayton, Wee wrote about his adventure for the *Mouse News*. "Wee Did It!" the headline exclaimed. Mice lined up to buy newspapers. Wee and his family worked long hours to print all the papers for their friends. They were pleased and tired that night when they went to bed.

Men had flown. A mouse had flown! Life would never be the same, Wee suspected. But, as he tucked in his little ones and snuggled into his nest with Mama, he felt sure one thing had not changed—it was a wonderful time to be a mouse.

ABOUT THE WRIGHT BROTHERS

Wilbur and Orville Wright lived in Dayton, Ohio. They had a brief career as printers and then operated a successful bicycle business. Long interested in flight, they realized the key to success was control. From 1900 through 1902, they built a series of gliders to test their ideas and flew them on North Carolina's Outer Banks at Kitty Hawk, a place with strong winds and soft sand. They built the engine-powered *Flyer* in 1903.

On December 14, Wilbur won a coin toss for the first flight. The sensitive craft leaped off the track, stalled, then dropped to the ground. Some damage to the *Flyer* and unfavorable weather delayed their next attempt until December 17. With Orville at the controls, the *Flyer* took off at 10:35 A.M. It flew for twelve seconds and traveled 120 feet over the ground. The Wrights made four flights that day, each one longer than the last. The final flight, with Wilbur piloting, lasted fifty-nine seconds and covered 852 feet.

Other people had tried to make flying machines, but no one knew how to steer a machine in the air. The Wright brothers realized that flying an airplane was like riding a bicycle—they needed to tilt and turn it to go where they wanted, including up and down. They made the wingtips twistable so they could tilt the plane from side to side. A rudder allowed them to point the plane's nose left or right. Using these controls together, the brothers could keep an airplane stable in gusty winds and steer it in any direction. Today, even the most advanced aircraft still use the Wright method of control.

ABOUT WEE THE MOUSE

Wee's story is fictional, but a mouse did share the Wright brothers' camp in 1902. Orville described how he had spent "whole days" building a trap for the mouse and baiting it with cornbread, only to find the cornbread gone and the trap empty. "My respect for the intelligence of that wee beastie has grown wonderfully the last week," he wrote years later.

Orville developed a grudging respect for "this one little beast, whose cunning has defeated every stratagem our ingenuity could devise." Any mouse that could outwit the inventors of the airplane must have been a clever creature indeed. Maybe it understood what Wilbur and Orville were up to. Maybe it dreamed of flying, too.

Henry Holt and Company, LLC, *Publishers since 1866*
115 West 18th Street, New York, New York 10011
www.henryholt.com

Henry Holt is a registered trademark of Henry Holt and Company, LLC
Text copyright © 2004 by Timothy R. Gaffney. Illustrations copyright © 2004 by Bernadette Pons.
All rights reserved. Distributed in Canada by H. B. Fenn and Company Ltd.
Library of Congress Cataloging-in-Publication Data
Gaffney, Timothy R.
Wee and the Wright brothers / Timothy R. Gaffney; illustrated by Bernadette Pons.
Summary: A rodent reporter from the "Mouse News" travels from Dayton, Ohio, to Kitty Hawk, North Carolina,
to cover Wilbur and Orville Wright's historic 1903 flight. 1. Wright, Wilbur, 1867–1912—Juvenile fiction.
2. Wright, Orville, 1871–1948—Juvenile fiction. [1. Wright, Wilbur, 1867–1912—Fiction.
2. Wright, Orville, 1871–1948—Fiction. 3. Flight—Fiction. 4. Mice—Fiction.] I. Pons, Bernadette, ill. II. Title.
PZ7.G1195We 2004   [E]—dc22   2003020999
ISBN 0-8050-7172-5 / EAN 978-0-8050-7172-6 / First Edition—2004 / Designed by Donna Mark
The artist used watercolors and pastels on watercolor paper to create the illustrations for this book.
Printed in the United States of America on acid-free paper. ∞
1   3   5   7   9   10   8   6   4   2

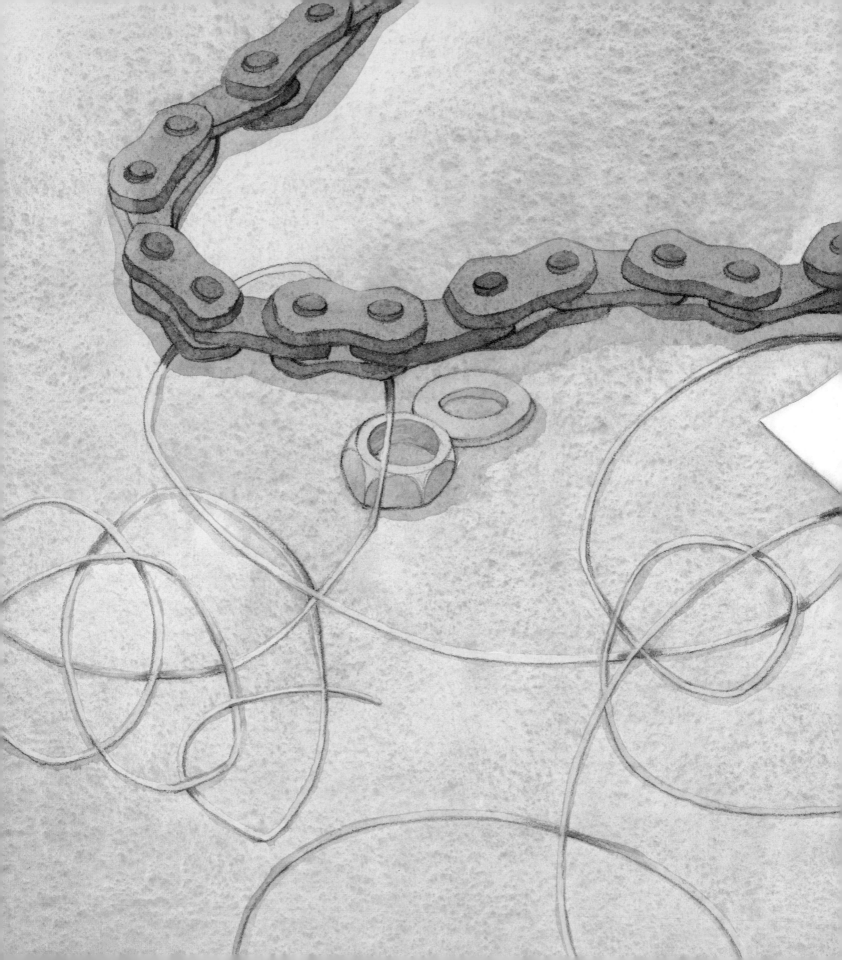